For Aunt Dot—B.P.

For Nathan—S.C.

Raintree is an imprint of Capstone Global Library Limited, a company incorporated in England and Wales having its registered office at 264 Banbury Road, Oxford, OX2 7DY – Registered company number: 6695582

www.raintree.co.uk
myorders@raintree.co.uk

Text © Capstone Global Library Limited 2019
The moral rights of the proprietor have been asserted.

ISBN 978 1 4747 6245 8
22 21 20 19 18
10 9 8 7 6 5 4 3 2 1

A CIP catalogue for this book is available from the British Library.

Designer: Lori Bye

Printed and bound in India

THE Picky EATER

written by Betsy Parkinson

illustrated by Shane Clester

Curious Fox
a capstone company-publishers for children

Piper is a wonderful piglet. She works hard in school. She can speak Latin fluently.

She is a great dancer.

And she is a
marvellous mud-roller.

But Piper is NOT a good eater. Some might call her picky, but Piper doesn't see it that way.

She has just one simple rule for her food:

It Must begin with the LetteR P.

At breakfast, she gets waffles,
eggs and orange juice.

"Nope! Not gonna eat it!" Piper exclaims.

Her mum calmly says,
"Please, eat five bites."

Piper eats exactly five bites.
"Waffles are not pancakes. The egg isn't poached.
And the orange juice has no pulp," she says.

At lunch, Piper is served a turkey sandwich,
an apple and a chocolate-chip cookie.

Her father says, "Please, my little piglet.
Eat five bites. Yum!"

Piper eats exactly five bites. She rolls her eyes.
"The apple is not a pear. The turkey should
be peanut butter. And pie would be
so much better than a cookie," she says.

At dinner, Piper is served rice,
green beans and chicken nuggets.

"Please, take just five bites," her parents plead.

Again, Piper takes exactly five bites.
"The rice is not pasta. The beans are not peas.
And I prefer pizza to chicken nuggets,"
she tells her parents.

Piper's mother didn't know what to do.
She ordered a book and followed its advice.
As she whipped up her pineapple
upside-down cake, she hid vegetables inside.

But Piper was not fooled.

How to get
your picky
PIGLET
to eat

The next night, as usual,
Piper objected to dinner. But this time,
Piper's mum was NOT in the mood
for another fight about food.

In fact, she lost her piggy marbles!

"Fine," she said to Piper. "Don't eat, but you may not utter a word or you'll be sent to your room."

"But!" replied Piper.

"Not. One. Word," said Piper's mum.

Piper just sat there.

Mum and Dad kept eating.

The next night, Piper quietly tried
some new food. She ate carrots, meatballs
and apples. She was full.

By Friday, Piper was quite hungry.
She took a bite. Then she took another bite.
Pretty soon, she had eaten a small dinner.

Piper kept sitting.

This happened every night that week.

"Well, I suppose I can eat food that doesn't begin with P," Piper told her parents. "But don't even think about messing with my **PINK** and **PURPLE** clothes!"